Dear Parent:
Your child's love of reading starts here!

Every child learns to read in a different way and at his or her own speed. Some go back and forth between reading levels and read favorite books again and again. Others read through each level in order. You can help your young reader improve and become more confident by encouraging his or her own interests and abilities. From books your child reads with you to the first books he or she reads alone, there are I Can Read Books for every stage of reading:

SHARED READING
Basic language, word repetition, and whimsical illustrations, ideal for sharing with your emergent reader

BEGINNING READING
Short sentences, familiar words, and simple concepts for children eager to read on their own

READING WITH HELP
Engaging stories, longer sentences, and language play for developing readers

READING ALONE
Complex plots, challenging vocabulary, and high-interest topics for the independent reader

I Can Read Books have introduced children to the joy of reading since 1957. Featuring award-winning authors and illustrators and a fabulous cast of beloved characters, I Can Read Books set the standard for beginning readers.

A lifetime of discovery begins with the magical words **"I Can Read!"**

Visit www.icanread.com for information
on enriching your child's reading experience.

Pete the Kitty: Ready, Set, Go-Cart!
Text copyright © 2021 by Kimberly and James Dean
Illustrations copyright © 2021 by James Dean
Pete the Kitty © 2015 by Pete the Cat, LLC
Pete the Kitty is a registered trademark of Pete the Cat, LLC, Registration Number 5576697

Library of Congress Control Number: 2020942278
ISBN 978-0-06-297405-1 (trade bdg.) — ISBN 978-0-06-297404-4 (pbk.)

21 22 23 24 CWM 10 9 8 7 6 5
❖
First Edition

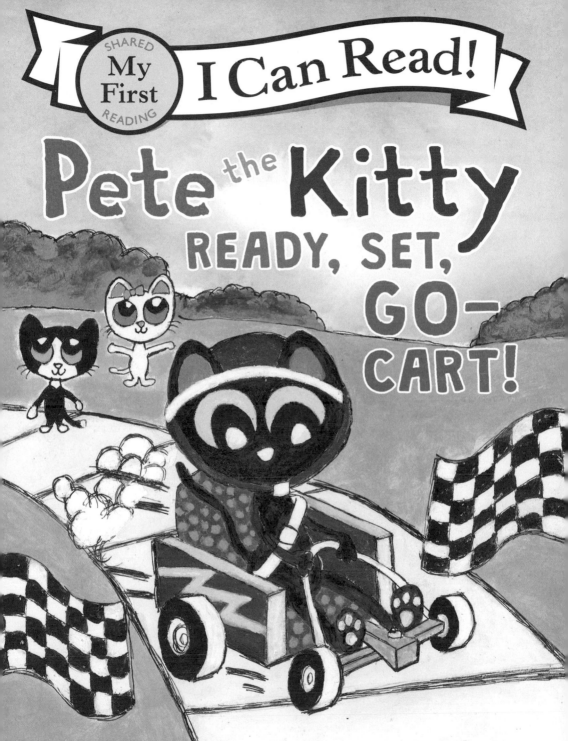

My First SHARED READING

I Can Read!

Pete the Kitty
READY, SET, GO—CART!

by Kimberly & James Dean

HARPER
An Imprint of HarperCollins Publishers

Pete loves go-carts.

Go-carts go fast.

Pete wants to make a go-cart.
He will make the fastest one!

Pete looks for a box.

He finds an old wooden box.

"This is perfect!" he says.

Pete sits in the box.

"Zoom!" says Pete.

But he can't see the road.

Something is missing.

"You need a seat!" says Bob.

Pete and Bob look for a seat.

Bob finds an old chair.

The chair is perfect!
They put the seat
in the go-cart.

Pete sits in the go-cart.

"Zoom!" says Pete.

But the go-cart does not go.

Something is missing.
"You need wheels!"
says Callie.

Pete, Bob, and Callie look
for wheels.
Callie finds an old wagon.

The wheels are perfect!
They put the wheels
on the go-cart.

The go-cart rolls a little.

"Zoom!" Pete says.

But Pete's go-cart is slow.

Something is missing.
"You will go fast
if you go down a hill,"
says Callie.

Pete and his pals
look for a hill.
Callie finds a tall hill.

Bob finds a taller hill.

Pete finds the tallest hill.

Pete and his pals
push the go-cart
up the hill.

Ready!

Set!

"Wait!" says Pete.

"Something is missing,"
says Pete.
"What?" asks Bob.

The go-cart
has a box.

The go-cart
has a seat.

The go-cart has wheels.

"My go-cart needs
cool colors!"
says Pete.

Pete paints cool lines
on the go-cart.
Now, Pete is ready to go fast!

Ready!

Set!

Go!

The go-cart starts to roll.

It rolls down the big hill.

Pete's go-cart goes fast.

His go-cart goes faster.

"Zoom!" says Pete.
His go-cart is the fastest!

Pete's pals cheer.

"You did it, Pete!"

"No," says Pete. "We did it!"

Pete loves his new go-cart.
But he loves his pals
most of all.